Sir Gadabout
Goes to Knight School

Other brilliant *Sir Gadabout* books
by Martyn Beardsley

Sir Gadabout
Sir Gadabout Gets Worse
Sir Gadabout and the Ghost
Sir Gadabout Does His Best
Sir Gadabout and the Little Horror
Sir Gadabout Goes Overboard
Sir Gadabout Goes Barking Mad

You can find out more about *Sir Gadabout* at
http://sirgadabout.mysite.freeserve.com/

Martyn Beardsley

Sir Gadabout

Goes to Knight School

Illustrated by Tony Ross

Orion
Children's Books

First published in Great Britain in 2006
by Orion Children's Books
a division of the Orion Publishing Group Ltd
Orion House
5 Upper St Martin's Lane
London WC2H 9EA

5 7 9 10 8 6 4

A catalogue record for this book
is available from the British Library

ISBN 10: 1-84255-276-7
ISBN 13: 978-1-84255-276-6

Printed in Great Britain by Clays Ltd, St Ives plc

The Orion Publishing Group's policy is to use papers that
are natural, renewable and recyclable products and made
from wood grown in sustainable forests. The logging and
manufacturing processes are expected to conform to the
environmental regulations of the country of origin.

www.orionbooks.co.uk

Thanks to Karen E. for the idea!

Contents

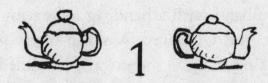

One Disaster Too Many

A long, long time ago, when mobile phones just rang instead of making strange noises or playing funny tunes, there was a castle called Camelot. It was a proud and mighty fortress, far away in the remotest western part of the land – although there were plenty of service stations along the way in case you needed the toilet or were dying for a drink.

And here lived King Arthur (in the castle, not one of the service stations. He never used them because he thought the food was too expensive. And as for needing the toilet: "Make sure you go before you set off" was his motto.) Where was I? Oh, yes, King

Arthur – a wiser and braver ruler there had never been. Guinevere was his queen, so beautiful that many a man's wife had belted her husband with a handbag for staring too much. And Guinevere was also pretty good at making things – she it was who added the conservatory at the back of Camelot. It was so well made that it still stands today, where it houses the National Trust's Interactive Guide to the Moths and Butterflies of Britain (entrance £5, free to members).

The knights of Camelot were skilful and brave. They sat at the famous Round Table, where they discussed how they could make the kingdom safe from dragons, villains, teapots in service stations which pour hot water all over the table instead of into the cup, and so on. The Camelot knights were known as the best in the world – at least, most of them were.

One seemed to have slipped in who was not quite up to standard. Some say he was a carpenter's assistant who got locked in one night while finishing off the Round Table

and then somehow managed to tag along with the rest of them. Others claim he was once a brilliant knight who was hit on the head by a monkey falling from a tree, and had never been the same since. Yet others say he *is* the monkey who fell from the tree, cleverly disguised as a knight. While still *others* say that no monkey could be as daft as Sir Gadabout – for he is the knight in question.

Sir Gadabout somehow managed to

remain a member of the Round Table despite being known as the Worst Knight in the World. Both King Arthur and Queen Guinevere were very fond of him because he always meant well, and anyway, things often turned out all right in the end.

But one day Sir Gadabout went too far, and it was decided that Something Must Be Done . . .

A few years previously, Sir Gadabout had accidentally set fire to the King of Gaul's beard at a royal 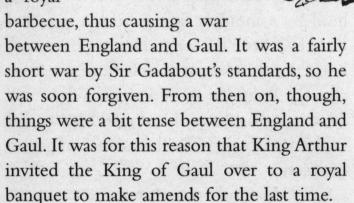 barbecue, thus causing a war between England and Gaul. It was a fairly short war by Sir Gadabout's standards, so he was soon forgiven. From then on, though, things were a bit tense between England and Gaul. It was for this reason that King Arthur invited the King of Gaul over to a royal banquet to make amends for the last time.

Even though King Arthur put Sir Gadabout in charge of the drinks to prevent him causing any more royal fires, on reflection it might have been better to have sent him well out of the way till the event was over.

Sir Gadabout decided to impress the guests by digging out his Aunty Scrofula's recipe for Summer Fizz. It was a delicious, refreshing drink and always went down well at parties. But the instructions for making it had been at the bottom of a drawer in Sir

Gadabout's room for ages among lots of other tatty old bits of paper. Without realising it, when he tried to piece together the pages for the Summer Fizz, Sir Gadabout also gathered up pages containing the instructions for Aunty Scrofula's Ant Exterminator mixture. The two recipes combined created a different sort of drink altogether . . .

The banquet was going very well, but it was a hot day and everyone was soon thirsty. Sir Gadabout had reserved his special Fizz for the honoured guests – and fizz it certainly did. Very soon, the King of Gaul's leading knight began running round in circles with steam billowing from his mouth, nose and ears. He eventually jumped into

Camelot's moat to cool off. Then a strange and rather disturbing smile spread across the face of the King of Gaul's brother, and he began to bound vigorously among the guests, claiming he was a kangaroo who could read people's minds. Worst of all, the King of Gaul's beard (only just fully regrown after the last Sir Gadabout incident) fell out in one go before everyone's eyes – along with his hair and eyebrows. He was quite short and round in shape anyway, and his hairless, shiny pink head now made him look rather like Humpty Dumpty.

It might easily have meant war again, but fortunately, once the party from Gaul had slept off the effects of the Fizz, they couldn't remember anything that had happened the previous day. In fact, many of them couldn't even remember their own names, which Guinevere solved by making little name badges for everyone to wear.

Everything was smoothed over, but it was a close run thing.

"I really think we have to do something

about Sir Gadabout," said King Arthur sadly to the Queen. "I don't *want* to kick him out of Camelot, but we simply can't afford any more disasters like this."

"I'm afraid I agree," Guinevere sighed. "I'd hate to see him go too, but I can't think what else we can do."

They didn't have the heart to sack him, so they tried to come up with other, nicer ways of getting rid of him: making him their Special Knight in China (but he would get lost on the way) or sending him on a long errand and moving Camelot brick by brick to another secret place while he was away (but that would take too long, and was still fairly cruel). They just couldn't think of anything other than telling him he had to pack his bags and leave, and they were very unhappy at the thought of it.

But just then, Sir Lancelot came along to give them his weekly report. He was a bit full of himself (though it had to be admitted that he genuinely was a great knight) and he had come to report how many dangerous dragons he had slain that week. Because he was so good, when Sir Lancelot wasn't out slaying dragons and winning battles, he was in charge of the Camelot School for Knights.

The school was really meant for youngsters who had shown promise and could be trained up to be full members of the Round Table. Sir Gadabout might not be young, and the only promise he showed was in starting wars with Gaul – but still . . .

King Arthur and Queen Guinevere looked at each other and smiled. "*That's it!*" they both cried. "Surely Sir Lancelot can teach him at least to be a *fairly* good knight? Then we won't have to sack him."

Even though when the plan was explained to Sir Lancelot he went away and wept quietly to himself for a while, it was quickly decided by royal decree . . . Sir Gadabout was going to Knight School!

2
Hair Today, Gone Tomorrow

Sir Gadabout soon received his instructions from King Arthur to report to the Camelot School for Knights. But the letter said that before he joined the school, he was to take the King of Gaul to get his memory restored – and if possible, his hair, too.

There was only one person who could do that.

On the way to see Merlin, the great wizard who had helped them on many previous adventures, Sir Gadabout and Herbert his faithful squire, were bombarded with questions from the King of Gaul.

"Where did you say I was the king of?"

"Goal, I think," replied Sir Gadabout. "I think you must have been a very good foot-baller or something."

"Wasn't he the King of Small?" wondered Herbert. "I think he might have ruled over a country of very little people."

"My word!" said the King. He rubbed his bald head. "And did I have hair once?"

"You certainly did," said Sir Gadabout. "And we are going to see someone who will be able to make it grow back for you – *as if by magic.*"

"Actually, it *is* by magic," Herbert pointed out.

"Oh, yes . . . Ah, here we are!"

The track had brought them to an old, mysterious cottage deep in the Willow Wood. They opened a gate and made their way along a winding path through an over-grown garden; but when they came to the door of the cottage, they found a large sign nailed to it saying: "NO ENTRY – SEE NEW DOOR ABOVE". There was a

ladder leaning against the wall, and it led up to where someone appeared to have drawn in chalk – not particularly well – a door in the wall of the cottage just below the roof.

"Ah, a new way in!" said Sir Gadabout. "Follow me, your majesty."

"But sire . . ." Herbert warned as he peered at the clumsy chalk lines above them.

However, Sir Gadabout was already leading the way up the ladder, quickly followed by the King of Small –

I mean, Gaul. His bald head was feeling pretty chilly and he was keen to get some hair back on it.

"Let's see if anyone's in," said Sir Gadabout, taking one hand off the top rung of the ladder and knocking loudly on the chalk door.

As soon as he did so, a strange figure appeared on the roof above them. He was wearing a blue and red uniform, and although he was rather turtlish in shape, the tight uniform made him look kind of spiderish – especially as he was leaning over the edge of the roof and holding on only by some double-sided sticky tape he had stuck to his hands and feet.

"Now I have you!" cried the spiderish-turtlish figure. "My goal is to make the world a safer place from villains and criminals. I shall capture you and hand you over to the authorities!"

"But, we were rather hoping to visit Merlin . . ." said Sir Gadabout.

But the spiderish-turtlish figure was already hurling a web in their direction, made of old bits of string and the remains of a ball of yellow wool that his mum had given him.

Unfortunately, he put so much effort into throwing his home-made web that the double-sided sticky tape proved not quite sticky enough.

"*Eeeek!*" he yelled as he came unstuck and shot off the edge of the roof.

Just when it appeared that he was going to fall to the floor and suffer all sorts of painful injuries, his web caught on Sir Gadabout's nose (which was a trifle long, as noses go). The spiderish-turtlish figure ended up on his back inside his own web, swinging to and fro from Sir Gadabout's hooter.

"Get off my ladder!" squawked the indignant not-so-super hero.

"*Get off by dose!*" cried Sir Gadabout, whose eyes were beginning to water.

"Dr McPherson – come down from there immediately!" ordered a new voice. This was Sidney Smith, Merlin's talking ginger cat. He often joined Sir Gadabout on his adventures, knowing it was usually good for a laugh or two.

Pretty soon, they had sorted the whole tangle out, and Sir Gadabout, Herbert and the King of Goal – sorry, Gaul – all went in to see the great wizard.

The inside of Merlin's cottage was dark and shadowy, lit only by flickering candles and one of those little desktop lamps from Ikea. Merlin himself was sitting at a large table. He was surrounded by dusty books of spells, bubbling potions in glass jars (although one of them was his cup of tea), and little boxes full of strange-smelling herbs. Merlin was tall (at least, he was when he was standing up) and thin, and wore a great dark cloak covered in little silver stars and moons. His hair was grey, long and straggly.

"What have we here?" asked the wizard in his deep voice when he saw the visitors.

"We have the King of Ball, Merlin," Sir Gadabout explained. "He rules over a land of very small footballers, er, I think. But anyway, due to an accident – which wasn't *all* my fault – he has lost his hair . . . and . . . and . . . what was the other thing?"

"His memory, sire," said Herbert.

"Ah, yes. King Arthur was hoping you might be able to help."

Merlin looked the King up and down and stroked his long grey beard. "Hmm, very well. Did he have a lot of hair?"

"Quite a lot," replied Sir Gadabout. "And with him being a proper king and everything, I think you should use your very strongest hair-restoring spell, please."

"Well," smiled Merlin. "I don't think you want the *strongest* one . . ."

"Oh, yes, definitely," Sir Gadabout insisted. "I mustn't get this wrong after all the trouble there's been."

"If you say so," said Merlin, blowing the dust from one of his spell books.

After a minute of reading and deep thought, he rose to his feet, raised his arms, and began to recite the spell:

> *By night and day*
> *By wind and water*
> *This man's hair*
> *Doesn't grow where it oughta*
>
> *By the sun and the moon*
> *And the light they show*
> *May the hair on his head*
> *Grow and grow!*

As he spoke the last words, Merlin clapped his bony hands together loudly, and all eyes turned on the King.

At first, nothing seemed to happen, and Sir Gadabout began to worry that even this spell wasn't strong enough. But soon, little hairs began to sprout out of the unfortunate man's shiny head. They grew and grew, and within only a few minutes he had a full head of hair – together with a splendid beard and moustache.

Merlin held up a mirror so that he could see.

"Excellent!" beamed the King.

"And now for his memory," said Merlin, turning over the pages of another spell book. "Let me see . . ." and he began to pour small amounts of liquid from the different jars and bottles on his desk into an empty mug.

"*Four drops of that . . . two-and-a-half ounces of this . . . five epigrams of that . . . a rat's bellyful of that . . .*" muttered Merlin as he worked. Finally, he stirred it all together and gave it to the King.

The King had to hold his flourishing new beard out of the way before he could drink

it – it was now longer than Merlin's – and he
gulped it all down in one go.

"How long will it take?" asked Sir
Gadabout.

"Restoring someone's memory isn't easy,"
said Merlin. "This will take a few minutes."

"*Flumph-umph-mumph!*" said a voice, but it
was so muffled and peculiar that everyone
thought it must be the wind outside.

"His majesty will be so pleased to get back
to normal!" said Herbert.

"*Flumph-umph-mumph!*"

"And King Arthur will be pleased with
me!" said Sir Gadabout. "I mean, *all* of us, of
course . . ."

"*Flumph-umph-mumph!*"

"What *is* that noise?" Sir Gadabout asked at last.

"I think you'll find it's your King of Ball," Merlin replied.

"GAUL!" screamed the King, finally managing to pull most of the hair out of his mouth. "I'M THE KING OF GAUL!"

"Excellent – his memory has returned," said Sir Gadabout.

"Er, but should he be quite that hairy?" Herbert wondered.

The King's hair was growing at an alarming rate, like a waterfall cascading from his head down his body.

There was a cat-like titter from a dark corner of the room.

"I did try to warn you . . ." said Merlin.

"Can't you just do a spell to stop it growing?" asked Sir Gadabout.

Merlin shook his head. "It's much too dangerous to put more than two powerful spells on a person in one day, I'm afraid."

There was side-splitting, cat-like laughter

from the same dark corner of the room.

"*Flumph-umph-mumph!*" said the King of Gaul, trying desperately to remove yet more hair from his mouth. His hair wouldn't stop growing and was already down to his waist. His fringe had gone past his eyes and was getting into his mouth, along with his moustache. His beard was nearly down to his knees. In fact, he was so hairy that he looked rather like a grizzly bear. On top of this, he had now recalled what had happened to

him at the banquet. And the banquet before that.

"I didn't quite catch that," said Sir Gadabout politely.

"I SAID," the King of Gaul roared, "THAT'S IT. I'M A PATIENT MAN, BUT YOU'VE PUSHED ME TOO FAR. I'M GOING TO COME BACK HERE WITH MY ARMY AND DESTROY THE LOT OF YOU!" And he stamped out of the room.

"Well, there was no need to shout," said Sir Gadabout.

"Some people are never happy, sire," said Herbert.

"*FLUMPH!*" cursed the King of Gaul as he tripped over his hair and banged his knee on his way out.

The New Teacher

Meanwhile, at the Camelot School for Knights, just a stone's throw from the castle itself, Sir Lancelot surveyed the rows of junior knights as they stood before him for morning inspection, their suits of armour shining in the sun. To see his smart young pupils in neat rows, their swords and other equipment in perfect order just as he had trained them, usually filled him with pride. In fact, a lot of things filled Sir Lancelot with pride, starting when he first saw himself in the mirror in the morning. But this particular morning was different.

The news that his precious school – famed

around the world for producing the most fearsome and bravest of knights – was about to enrol the Worst Knight in the World, had left him feeling depressed and miserable. *Things* happened when Sir Gadabout was around. Horrible things. Embarrassing things. Disastrous things. In fact, Sir Gadabout would have started yesterday if he hadn't mistaken a watering can for his helmet and then got it stuck fast on his head. Sir Lancelot heard that he had set off anyway for the School for Knights,

which was only round the corner from Camelot, but had last been heard of in the region of Argyll and Bute, asking bewildered Scottish folk for directions

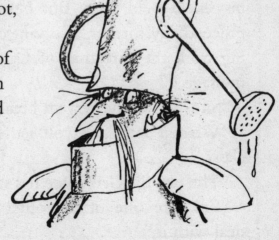

down the spout of a watering can.

Pulling himself together, Sir Lancelot began today's lesson.

"You will remember that yesterday," he said to his pupils, "we learned how to creep up on a troll guarding a bridge. But things don't always go to plan – what if he spots you before you get close? Trolls are very powerful creatures and often carry an axe, which will be much longer than your sword. What can we do?"

To demonstrate, Sir Lancelot picked out one pupil to play the part of the troll, drew his sword, and began to approach with his shield held high. But before he could proceed any further, a servant came scurrying from the direction of Camelot with a message.

"Sire!" cried the servant breathlessly.

"What is it? Can't you see I'm taking a class?"

"The evil Sir Grievance has struck again!"

"I'm sure one of the other knights can deal with it."

"But sire, Sir Tristran's back's gone again and Sir Gawain's got to wait in for the gas man. King Arthur's very worried because Sir Grievance has carried off Lady Belinda and is going to force her to marry him!"

"I am very busy . . . Erm, is she the one who is known as Belinda the Beautiful?"

"I think so, sire."

"Well, I might be able to spare a day or two. Class, I have taught you that a knight must always go to the aid of anyone in distress without hesitation. Since Belinda the – er, Lady Belinda – is in need of my help, I must depart immediately. Sir Grievance is a cunning man and I may be detained, so in the meantime I shall arrange for King Arthur to send another knight to continue teaching you. Farewell!"

In fact, Sir Lancelot's mind was so full of Belinda the Beautiful that he completely forgot about getting someone to cover for him. He headed straight for Sir Grievance's castle among the Mournful Mountains, and was gone for several days.

For a while, the junior knights carried on with the lesson, taking it in turns to be the troll guarding the bridge and the knight trying to defeat him. When that got boring they had a game of football – which isn't easy in suits of armour (though it doesn't hurt so much when you get fouled).

Later, just when they were beginning to think they might as well go home for the day, the pupils were brought to a standstill by a loud noise. It was a tremendous crash, combined with the sound of clanking and breaking armour.

"I thought that was a gate . . ." the junior knights heard a distant groggy voice say.

"That's a fence, sire," said another voice. "The gate's just a bit further along. Er . . . it's open, sire."

"Well, you'd think there'd be a sign or something."

"I'll set to work painting a couple with my tail immediately," said a sarcastic cat-like voice. "Something along the lines of: 'This is a fence – do not walk into it' and 'This is a gate – it opens and closes'." (Thus proving what a clever cat Sidney Smith was, since modern health and safety regulations do now recommend such signs.)

When Sir Gadabout – for it was he – limped through the gate of the School for Knights, busily trying to fix bits of armour back into place which had come off during his recent mishap, the pupils had a quick discussion among themselves.

"It must be our new teacher," said one.

"But it's Sir Gadabout! I mean, *Sir Gadabout!*" cried another.

"Well, he is still a knight of the Round Table. He must be able to teach us *something*."

"But why is he wearing a watering can on his head?"

Algernon, the head pupil, was sent to greet the new arrival. He strode up to Sir Gadabout, but unfortunately he was still wielding his sword from a practice session.

"AAARGH, WE'RE UNDER ATTACK! RUN FOR YOUR LIVES!" screamed Sir Gadabout, turning to flee. Unfortunately, he was tripped over by one of his own pieces of dangling leg armour. He fell flat on his face and the spout of the watering can buried itself deep in the ground, making it impossible for him to get up.

Poor Algernon looked aghast at the

accident he seemed to have caused, and quickly sheathed his sword.

"He comes in peace," Sidney Smith reassured Sir Gadabout.

"Sir Lancelot was teaching us how to deal with trolls," said Algernon, helping Herbert, to prise the knight's watering-can spout from the ground. "But now that he's been called away, we're ready and willing to learn everything we can from you!"

"Looks like they think you're the new teacher!" tittered Sidney Smith down the spout of the watering can.

"What are you laughing at, you scrawny rat-catcher?" said Herbert, who always hated it when the cat made fun of his master. "Sir Gadabout can teach these young 'uns a thing or two!"

"Sure, like how to poison the King of Gaul."

They were interrupted by a sound like the popping of a cork from a bottle. Sir Gadabout had finally managed to yank the watering can from his head, and he smiled red-faced but proudly at Algernon. "If the School for Knights needs a teacher, then Sir Gadabout is at your service!"

Sidney Smith looked at the rows of young trainee knights who had lined up to greet their new teacher and clapped a paw to his head. "So young, yet their careers already ruined."

The Mystery Pupil

For his first lesson in charge of the Camelot School for Knights, Sir Gadabout strode grandly up and down before the rows of eager young pupils.

"Ah," he smiled. "This takes me back to my days in the school!"

"You mean *day*," Sidney Smith pointed out. "You poked the instructor in the eye with your spear, injured half the pupils trying to get away from a bee, and demolished the main school building when your horse ran wild with you on it!"

"The bee got under his saddle," explained Sir Gadabout calmly. He turned back to the class. "Now, I'm sure that Sir Lancelot will already have gone through the basics with you, but you might be surprised what tips you can pick up from different knights. Take the trusty sword . . ."

He removed his sword from its scabbard to reveal a rather rusty blade that was broken in the middle and held together by sticky tape. "Now, you might think that a sword that is stuck together like this would be useless – but no! It has all sorts of uses."

He demonstrated a few jabs and swishes with his sword. After one particularly dramatic *swish*, the end of the sword came flying off – and carried on swishing in the direction of the students, where it clanged across several helmets like Big Ben chiming the hour.

"Er, for example," said Sir Gadabout hurriedly, "you can attack opponents who are far away – like that. Or you could do that to someone who had a longer weapon than you, like, umm . . ."

"A troll!" cried one bright pupil who had

remembered his earlier lesson.

"*A troll – where?*" squealed Sir Gadabout, looking all around in panic. "A TROLL! RUN AWAY!"

It took all of Herbert's considerable strength to drag his master back, while at the same time whispering quietly in his ear.

"Ah!" said Sir Gadabout when he discovered the truth. "You see – one method is to pretend to be afraid and run away, then hide behind a bush and jump out at your enemy as he chases after you!"

"How many knights do that?" asked one pupil.

"Well, probably not many," Sir Gadabout replied.

"*Exactly* how many?" insisted the pupil, who was the only one carrying a notebook and scribbling information into it furiously.

"Maybe two or three . . . Does Sir Bors de Ganis still do it?" Sir Gadabout asked Herbert.

"He stopped doing it when he was eleven, sire."

"Hmm. Possibly only me, then."

"Thank you," said the note-taking pupil. "And while we're on the same subject, sire, is it true that a key to the Camelot drawbridge is left outside under a plant pot?"

"*Is* that the same subject?" wondered Sir Gadabout.

"No," Sidney Smith commented. He had been eyeing the star pupil suspiciously since he had noticed a sketch map of Camelot on an open page of the young knight's notebook.

Sir Gadabout shrugged his shoulders. "Anyway, yes, it's true—"

"*Sssh!*" urged the cat. But Sir Gadabout was hard to stop once he'd got going.

"Just in case any knights come back late at night, or the man on the drawbridge has gone for a cup of tea or something, we leave a spare key under a plant pot. It's quite safe — I'm sure no one would think of looking there. But *don't tell anyone!*"

When the class had finished for the day and the pupils were returning to their quarters (Guinevere had been in charge of rebuilding them bigger and better than before, after Sir Gadabout had destroyed the old building), Sidney Smith managed to have a quiet word with Alergnon, the head boy.

"Who is that knight who asks all the questions and takes all the notes?"

"Oh, Sir Lancelot calls him his Star Pupil.

He always takes a great interest in everything – not only how to be a knight, but all about Camelot and where the sentries live, what time they change over, that sort of thing. His name is William of Luag."

What neither Algernon nor Sidney Smith knew was that a great army was hidden in the forests near Camelot. The King of Gaul's memory of what had happened to him had finally returned (which meant he could throw his name badge away at last). In fury, he had brought over the mightiest army ever assembled, and he was watching and waiting for his moment to strike. Meanwhile, his best spy was already at work . . .

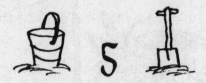

Sir Lancelot Returns

Over the next few days, Sir Gadabout continued to mould the country's brightest young knights into versions of himself. The pupils found it strange at first – especially since so many of the things he taught seemed to be the exact opposite of what they had learned from Sir Lancelot. But they had to admit it was more fun the Gadabout way, and they soon took to it with great enthusiasm.

For example, if another knight was charging fast and pointing his long spear straight at you in a dangerous manner, they found that it was much more exciting to

follow Sir Gadabout's advice and hang upside down from your horse till he'd gone past (even though it meant you couldn't get at him either – and the blood tended to rush to your head).

If your opponent seemed very skilful with his sword (as most did compared with Sir Gadabout), what better defence than to try to talk him into a game of hide-and-seek, where he has to close his eyes and count to a million, thus giving you plenty of time to get away? Sir Gadabout proudly told them

that a few years ago he had played that trick on Sir Malcolm the Malicious. Not only had it worked, but it was rumoured that the evil knight was still trying to count to a million. (He wasn't very good with numbers and kept losing his place and having to start again – but he was a very determined man.)

Before long, the pupils at the Camelot School for Knights had forgotten everything Sir Lancelot had ever taught them, and had turned into budding young Sir Gadabouts.

"The future of the Round Table is going to be very interesting," smirked Sidney Smith as he watched a pupil trying to throw a bent spear (just like Sir Gadabout's) at a target. It missed the target by quite some distance and went whizzing round and round, just like when you blow up a balloon then let it go. It narrowly missed a startled blackbird, whisked a sausage sandwich out of Herbert's hand just as he was going to take a bite, and finally pinned William of Luag to the wooden wall of the school by his collar.

The sandwich was dangling right under his nose and making his mouth water.

ℌas developed <u>highly dangerous</u> Secret Weapon

William scribbled in his busy notebook.

Even Herbert looked worried when he watched Sir Gadabout trying to teach the smallest young knight how to sword fight. At one point the boy waved his sword suddenly and made Sir Gadabout jump. (In fact, Sir Gadabout jumped so high that he landed on the roof of the school, accidentally breaking the World High Jump Record set only the previous week by the great Russian, Upannova, in the process. Sir Gadabout's record stands to this day, although the athletics people don't like to admit it.)

ħas deveſoped <u>amazing</u> physicaſ powers

William of Luag noted.

After a number of days of this (although one of those was an Inset Day so there were no lessons) and with the pupils now fully trained in Sir Gadabout's own special methods, news came through that Sir Lancelot was on his way back. He had beaten the evil Sir Grievance and his men single-handedly, and carried Belinda the Beautiful back to her family in triumph.

At about the same time, most of the Knights of the Round Table were leaving Camelot for their summer holidays. They had heard about a special "Two Knights for the Price of One" offer at the Sandy Beach Holiday Camp in Dawlish Warren, and had

packed their bags and buckets and spades and set off in a happy, holiday mood. (They also packed their own sandwiches so they didn't have to pay service station prices for food on the way.)

Knowing that it was Sir Gadabout's last day, the pupils at the Camelot School for Knights had clubbed together and bought him a card and a box of chocolates. When Algernon presented them to him, a tear came to Sir Gadabout's eye. This was because he had accidentally prodded his toe with his sword – but he was still very moved by the card and present.

When Sir Lancelot arrived to take charge of his school once more, Sir Gadabout told him how much he had enjoyed working with his pupils. "They're a fine bunch of lads," he said. "You'll be pleased to hear I've taught them everything I know."

"*That* didn't take long," Sidney Smith commented.

In fact, Sir Lancelot seemed quietly disheartened to hear that Sir Gadabout had taught them everything he knew, although he tried to hide his worst fears.

"And they gave me this," Sir Gadabout continued, showing Sir Lancelot his card. "They've all signed it . . . wait a minute. All except William of Luag . . ."

"Where *is* he, anyway?" Herbert wondered.

"Up to no good, if you ask me," said Sidney Smith.

"As soon as he heard that most of the knights had gone away on holiday, he just seemed to disappear, sire," Algernon told them.

"Gone on holiday?" exclaimed Sir Lancelot. "I thought I saw them preparing for battle with someone in the forest near Camelot as I was making my way back."

"No," Sir Gadabout explained. "They've gone to Dawlish Warren. I wouldn't have minded going myself. There's one of those curly-wurly slides that drops you into the water! Mind you, the last time I went on one my armour got stuck against the sides half way down and they had to fetch a man with a hammer and chisel to get me out—"

"Then who were those knights I saw in the forest?" pondered Sir Lancelot. "And where is William of Luag? *This could mean trouble!*"

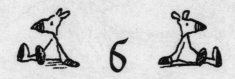

The Enemy at the Gates

King Arthur was woken from a pleasant sleep early the next morning by cries of alarm from the lookouts high in the towers of Camelot.

Far in the distance, a huge army on the march had been spotted. The early morning sun was glinting off their helmets and swords – and they were heading this way!

King Arthur carefully placed his teddy (called Humphrey Humbug) on his pillow, and without even bothering to change out of his pyjamas he rushed out to where Sir Lancelot and Queen Guinevere were already waiting for him.

Sir Gadabout had been woken at the same time by all the commotion. He had carefully placed *his* teddy (called Sir Teddybout – Sir Gadabout wasn't very good at thinking up names) and went rushing outside, also still in his pyjamas.

"It's a really big army, your majesty," one of the lookouts was telling the King when Sir Gadabout arrived. "And their flags and banners have a golden lion on a blue background."

"*The King of Gaul!*" cried King Arthur. "What am I to do? Nearly all the Knights of the Round Table are enjoying themselves on the beach at Dawlish Warren!"

"And on the curly-wurly slide!" Sir Gadabout pointed out helpfully. "I hope they remember to take their armour off first though . . ."

"There just aren't enough knights left to defend Camelot," cried the King. "By the time we get word to those on holiday, it will be too late. What can be done?"

"You could install a curly-wurly slide that whizzes all the way round Camelot!" suggested Sir Gadabout. "Then in future we wouldn't need to go on holiday and leave the castle unguarded. Oh, and it could drop you with a big *splash* into the moat. And we could have lots and lots of sand around the castle so it looks like a beach—" Sir Gadabout was beginning to get excited, but King Arthur was too worried to listen.

"That's no good *now*!"

"What about my pupils from the Camelot School for Knights?" said Sir Lancelot.

"They're very young," said the King doubtfully.

"But they are trained to the very highest

standards!" replied Sir Lancelot proudly.

"That's what you think, mate," sniggered Sidney Smith, who had turned up with Herbert.

"Well, there's no one else," said the King. "We have no choice. Go and get them ready."

"And I've got a few ideas," said Guinevere. "Just let me have the use of all the royal servants, and plenty of hammers and nails!"

"Oh dear," said Sir Gadabout. "I don't think the servants will run away, your majesty – there's no need to nail them down."

"That's not the plan," smiled Guinevere with a wink. Sir Gadabout wasn't sure what she meant, but Guinevere had never winked at him before and he blushed bright red anyway.

By now, the cloud of dust being raised by the approaching army could clearly be seen by all in Camelot, and preparations to meet them were being hastily made. The pupils from the knight school were quickly

marched to defend the castle (although Sir Lancelot couldn't understand why his pupils were skipping along instead of marching in a soldierly fashion), and lots of hammering and banging could be heard coming from the castle workshops.

Sir Gadabout and King Arthur hurried for their armour, swords and shields, and even Herbert armed himself with a big stick, while Sidney Smith sharpened his claws till they were like razor blades.

When the two forces finally came face to face in a field beneath the walls of Camelot, it seemed that there could only be one winner. The King of Gaul had thousands of knights, rows and rows of fierce warriors on horseback and on foot, just waiting for the order to charge. King Arthur had just about a hundred junior knights, a few old ones (they thought Dawlish Warren sounded too lively, and had stayed behind) and an assortment of servants. And Sir Gadabout. In his

hurry to get ready, Sir Gadabout had somehow managed to come out wearing his
pyjamas outside his armour, and he had
hastily picked up a saucepan lid instead of his
shield.

Guinevere had done her best. Not only
had she used lots of old tin cans to knock up
pretend armour so that the kitchen staff
could look like knights, she had also created
quite a few full-sized model knights made
of cardboard, with armour and faces painted
on. These were cleverly placed at the back,
and also high up along the ramparts of the
castle, so that from a distance they made
the army look bigger than it really was.

Sir Gadabout had even brought Sir
Teddybout along. He had stuck a pencil
under his arm for a spear and tied him to the
back of Sir Lancelot's dog, Growler, to make
him look like another knight. Unfortunately,
he didn't look even a teensy bit like a
knight. And anyway, when Growler rolled
over and wriggled on his back to scratch
an itch, Sir Teddybout soon came off.

Growler trotted away, attracted by the smells from Camelot's unguarded kitchens, and Sir Teddybout was left dangling on the end of the pencil, which had stuck in the grass.

"Ha!" shouted one of the enemy knights, seeing this. "They are falling already and we haven't even started!"

"Your majesty!" King Arthur called to the King of Gaul. "I'm sure we can sort this out peacefully. We should be friends, not enemies! Simply let me know what it is that has upset you, and I will make amends."

"What has upset me?!" spluttered the King of Gaul, whose long flowing hair was being gathered into a wheelbarrow by a specially trained boy who followed behind. "Every time I come to visit you as a guest you make me feel welcome. But *then* you set your special agent to secretly poison me. To set fire to my beard. To make me forget who I am. To make my hair keep growing so that I have to have it cut twenty times a day. And you ask why I am upset?"

"But he's not a special agent being wicked," the King tried to explain.

"He's just being Sir Gadabout being Sir Gadabout!" chortled Sidney Smith.

"I don't care what his name is. Now it's *my* turn to do horrible things to you." He turned to his men. "Army of Gaul: PREPARE TO ATTACK!"

"*Oo-er!*" exclaimed Sir Gadabout, looking round for a good place to hide.

The Battle Begins

Just as the vast army of Gaul was about to attack, a shower of arrows came whistling from the battlements of the castle and made them duck down. There may have only been cardboard soldiers lining the walls above, but Guinevere had cunningly come up with a machine that could pull back the strings of many bows all at once. It only took one person to run along fixing the arrows in place, and then press a lever which set them all off at the same time.

"I thought you said they'd all gone on to Dawlish Warren?" the King of Gaul asked William of Luag, plucking an arrow from his bushy beard (his mass of hair was proving a quite useful protective layer on top of his armour). Of course, the spy's name wasn't really William of Luag – he had changed it around to keep his identity a secret. It was really Mailliw of Gaul (they had strange names in Gaul back then).

"They *have* gone to Dawlish Warren; trust me, your majesty," said Mailliw.

"Ooh – isn't that the place with the curly-wurly water slide?" asked another of the knights.

"Stop gossiping and get fighting," bellowed the King. "CHAAARGE!"

The thunder of hooves was like an earthquake as the army of Gaul spurred on their horses and galloped towards the knight school pupils.

Sir Lancelot was at the head of his young knights. "Right, lads," he said in a determined voice. "Get a good grip on your shields, and on my command—"

But Algernon knew what to do at moments like this after his training with Sir Gadabout.

"Sharp pointy spears coming this way – RUN FOR YOUR LIVES!!"

"What on earth . . ." gasped Sir Lancelot, who suddenly found himself facing the whole charging enemy army alone.

But the knights of Gaul were used to fighting enemies who would charge back at them, not dodge out of the way. They were going so fast that they couldn't stop or change direction, and many of them crashed straight into the walls of the castle. One poor knight's spear hit the wall with such a clang that all of his armour rattled like a madman

playing a xylophone, and fell off piece by piece. He wandered dizzily away in his vest and underpants. Others drove their spears deep between the stones of the wall, and were left hanging there as their horses fled in panic. Sir Lancelot was such a brilliant knight that he easily fought off the ones that came his way.

"It looks like they've thought up a new way of fighting, your majesty," said the King of Gaul's general. "Perhaps we should be careful . . ."

"Nonsense!" cried the King. "They're just cowards. *Nobody* sets my beard on fire and gets away with it. We shall charge at the group around the King himself – and I'll take the lead!"

Around King Arthur were only a few of the old knights, together with Sir Lancelot, Sir Gadabout and Co., and the cardboard models made by Guinevere. Such was the King of Gaul's temper that he led the fastest charge on horseback there had ever been. So swiftly did they attack that King Arthur and his men could feel the wind from their approach. In fact, before the two sides came together that same wind lifted up the cardboard knights and sent them swooping and gliding over the heads of the enemy.

"ARRRGH – MAGIC KNIGHTS!" came a cry.

"Merlin the great wizard must be with them," said the King of Gaul. "I thought Mailliw said *he* was in Dawlish Warren with the rest of them?"

"He is, your majesty!" said Mailliw. "Don't

71

stop now!" (And in fact at that very moment Merlin was taking part in a treasure hunt around the Sandy Beach holiday camp, trying hard to resist the temptation to use his magic so that he could win.)

But all the running away and the supposedly magic knights had thrown the army of Gaul into confusion. People were racing around all over the place and shouting, and some of the King of Gaul's men were even attacking each other by mistake.

The pupils from the knight school were doing their best. Algernon was riding around hanging beneath his horse, poking at people with his spear from below. A youth called Crispin had perfected the Sir Gadabout Scream of Fear so well that it set the enemy's teeth on edge and no one would go near him. And two strapping young identical twins, both called Tim and hailing from Double Gloucester, had devised a very clever plan. One would fall down when attacked and pretend he had been killed, only for the other (who, of course, looked exactly like him) to leap out from behind a bush claiming to be the ghost of the dead knight come to haunt his killer. Many of the King of Gaul's knights fled from the battle shaking with fear at this trick and were never seen again.

Sir Gadabout ran through the crowd waving his sword — although only so he could get away — when he came across a familiar face.

"*You!*" cried Sir Gadabout.

"*You!*" cried Mailliw of Gaul.

"Take that," said Sir Gadabout, thrusting forward with his sword. For once in his life, his sword actually did hit his opponent – but it broke in the middle where it was held together by sticky tape. The pointy bit of the blade fell harmlessly to the ground, and Sir Gadabout carried on plunging forward and bumped his nose on Mailliw of Gaul's armour.

"Take that!" said Mailliw of Gaul, slashing viciously at Sir Gadabout with his sword.

The blade sliced down the front of Sir Gadabout's pyjamas, and all the buttons

came pinging off. One hit Mailliw of Gaul on the nose, one in the eye and one went into his gaping mouth. "Take that!" said Sir Gadabout.

"Take that," said Mailliw of Gaul, swiping

his sword in the direction of Sir Gadabout's neck. Sir Gadabout raised his shield — only to realise for the first time that he was holding a puny saucepan lid which couldn't possibly keep a heavy sword at bay. Just when it seemed certain that Sir Gadabout's head would be chopped off, the sword was knocked from Maiiliw of Gaul's hand by a blow from a stout piece of wood.

"Take that!" said Herbert.

Before Herbert could do any more damage with his big stick, Mailliw of Gaul took flight, and soon became lost in the crowd of fighting knights.

The battle swung one way then the other. At times there were just so many knights in the army from Gaul that they threatened to overpower King Arthur and his defenders at any moment. But with Sir Lancelot in the thick of it, sending his opponents flying left, right and centre, and with Guinevere's special arrow-firing machine at work up on the battlements, they were just managing to hold on.

But the Camelot people were tiring. Every time they fought off one attack, there were always more knights to replace the beaten ones. King Arthur knew they couldn't hold on for ever – it seemed they almost needed a miracle to survive.

And then a cry went up that changed everything.

"LOOK! THE KNIGHTS OF THE ROUND TABLE ARE RETURNING!"

There was a sudden hush over the battle-field as all heads turned, and sure enough, moving through the forest could be seen the glinting silver armour of many knights heading their way.

A great cheer went up from the Camelot defenders. Sir Gadabout's voice was so loud that it almost drowned out the rest of them – but that was only because someone's horse had run over his foot.

There was a groan of despair from the knights of Gaul. If they couldn't beat the little army in front of them, what chance would they stand against the formidable Knights of the Round Table? Despite all the King of Gaul's pleading, his army quickly melted away.

But the King himself remained defiant. He climbed down from his horse and stood with his sword and shield, ready to take on the whole of Camelot alone if necessary. He bravely waited for the Knights of the Round

Table to emerge from the forest, while his boy valiantly remained behind to gather up his ever-growing hair into the wheel-barrow.

8

The Secret Army

What emerged from the forest was not an army of Knights of the Round Table at all. It was a very long plank of wood, carried by Guinevere at one end, Herbert at the other, and Sidney Smith in the middle. Nailed to the plank was an equally long row of spare suits of armour, and a lot of old swords dangling down, tied to the wood with string and clanking against the armour as the three of them moved forwards.

When the King of Gaul saw that he had been tricked again, he dropped his sword, sank slowly to the ground, and burst into tears.

"I've tried!" he wept. "Heaven knows, I've tried. But every time I come here it always ends up the same. *I hate this place!*"

It was very sad to see the proud King of Gaul blubbering away like this, especially when none of it was really his fault.

Sir Gadabout went up and quietly offered the King his handkerchief, but he refused it, saying it probably had poison in it knowing *them*. To be fair to the King, Sir Gadabout did have a bad cold and so it wasn't exactly a *clean* handkerchief. It did in fact look as

though it might have just a little poison of some kind in it.

It was Guinevere who managed to finally cheer the King of Gaul up a bit. She went over to him and put her arm round his shoulders.

"There, there," she said.

"It's just not *fair!*" the King of Gaul snivelled.

"I know, I know. What's your name? It doesn't seem very friendly to keep calling you the King of Gaul!"

"It's Bonebag."

"That's a nice name." (Which was only a tiny white lie. And it was in a good cause.)

Guinevere apologised to Bonebag for all the trouble they had caused him. She explained all about the Aunty Scrofula's Summer Fizz and Aunty Scrofula's Ant Exterminator problem, and how that and everything else had all been a series of unfortunate mistakes.

Eventually, the King of Gaul's temper improved, and King Arthur and Queen

Guinevere invited him to a grand banquet at Camelot to make up for what had happened. The thought of another banquet at Camelot had a strange effect on the King of Gaul. Gazing at Sir Gadabout, his face went deathly pale, and his left eye twitched as though there was something in it.

But Guinevere promised him that there would be delicious food, drink, and beautiful music. In particular, she *promised* that Sir Gadabout would sit quietly, well away from the King, and not make any drinks or start any fires.

And so it was that the King of Gaul – after Merlin had finally got his hair sorted out – was guest of honour at the most splendid banquet that Camelot had ever laid on. The food was scrumptious, the music delightful, and before long the King was having such a marvellous time that he could even laugh at some of the tricks that had been played on him during the battle.

"That arrow-firing machine was amazing!" he said to Guinevere. "Did you build it all by yourself?"

"I had some help from the servants," she replied modestly. "It was the long piece of wood with all the armour on that I built by myself."

"I held the heaviest end," said Herbert. "But being pretty strong I didn't feel tired at all, even after walking all the way through the forest with it."

"It probably seemed heavy because I was sitting on it, not really helping to carry it," chuckled Sidney Smith.

"But I doubt whether we could have lasted so long without my highly trained knight school pupils," Sir Gadabout shouted. (He had to shout because he had been placed at the far end of the long table, well away from the King of Gaul.)

Sir Lancelot, who had been enjoying himself so much that he had forgotten about what had become of his precious students while he had been away, had to go to his room and lie down for a while when he heard this.

And even though, in standing up to shout, Sir Gadabout had knocked his candle off the table and it was rolling unnoticed along the floor in the direction of the King of Gaul's magnificent long velvet trousers, I won't go into what happened next. It's always best for a story to have a happy ending.

It's enough just to say that Sir Gadabout was still – by *miles* – the Worst Knight in the World.